ADLERMAN BOOKS

Africa Calling, Nighttime Falling
Hey, Diddle Diddle
Humpty Dumpty
Rock-a-bye Baby
Songs for America's Children
How Much Wood Could a Woodchuck Chuck?
Oh No, Domino!
Mommy's Having a Watermelon
Rub a Dub Dub
A Toucan Can Can You?

BY KIN EAGLE

(Danny and Kim's pen name)

It's Raining, It's Pouring

ADLERMAN MUSIC

One Size Fits All
Listen UP!
...and a Happy New Year
(with Kevin Kammeraad and Yosi)

ADLERMAN GAMES

Compound It All!

illustrated by

Lindsay Barrett George • Megan Halsey

Ashley Wolff • Demi • Ralph Masiello

Wendy Anderson Halperin

Kevin Kammeraad • Pat Cummings

Dar (Hosta) • Leeza Hernandez

Christee Curran-Bauer

Kim Adlerman • Symone Banks

music by **Jim Babjak**

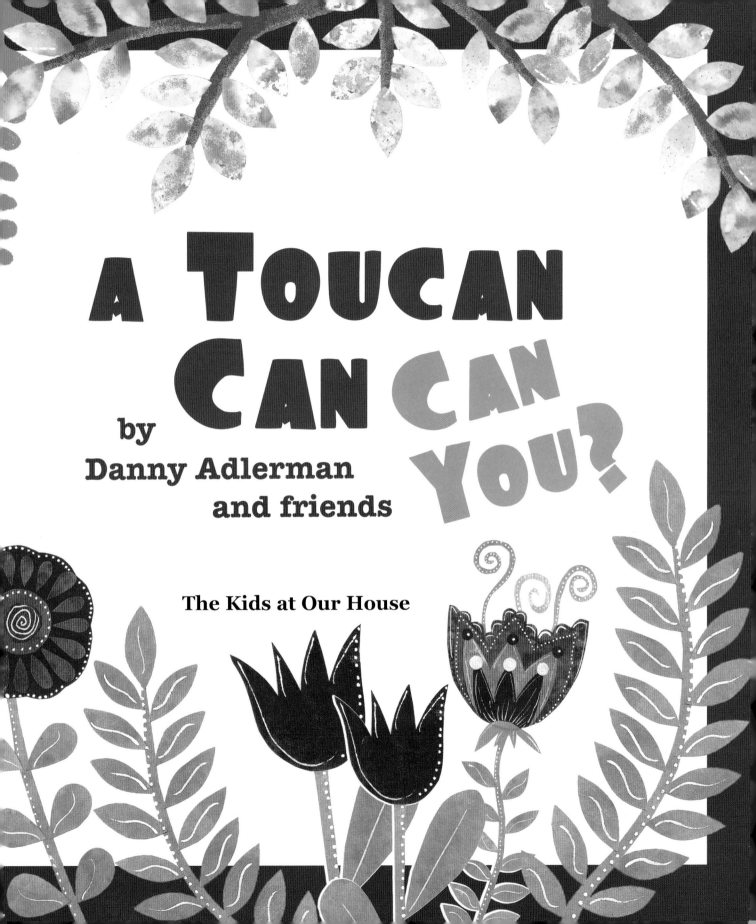

A Toucan Can Can You?

by
**Danny Adlerman
and friends**

The Kids at Our House

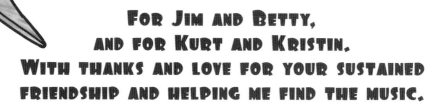

FOR JIM AND BETTY,
AND FOR KURT AND KRISTIN.
WITH THANKS AND LOVE FOR YOUR SUSTAINED
FRIENDSHIP AND HELPING ME FIND THE MUSIC.

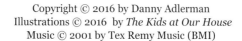

The Kids at Our House
47 Stoneham Place, Metuchen, NJ 08840
www.dannyandkim.com   info@dannyandkim.com
Like us on Facebook: Danny and Kim and friends

10 9 8 7 6 5 4 3 2 1 (h c)
10 9 8 7 6 5 4 3 2 1 (s c)

Printed in China by Jade Productions.
Book production and design by *The Kids at Our House*.
The display type was set in Foo.

The border image for the illustration of the Spaceship spread is of the Milky Way, over Northern Michigan, taken in late fall 2013 by Gary Appold, Emmet County IT Director, at the Headlands International Dark Sky Park in Mackinaw City, Emmet County, Michigan.

**Publisher's Cataloging-in-Publication
(Provided by Quality Books, Inc.)**

Adlerman, Daniel, 1963-
    A toucan can can you? / by Danny Adlerman and friends ; illustrated by Lindsay Barrett George, Megan Halsey, Ashley Wolff, Demi, Ralph Masiello, Wendy Anderson Halperin, Kevin Kammeraad, Pat Cummings, Dar (Hosta), Leeza Hernandez, Christee Curran-Bauer, Kim Adlerman, Symone Banks ; music by Jim Babjak.
        pages cm
    SUMMARY: Compound word play with corresponding illustrations.
        Audience: Ages 6-10.
    ISBN 978-1-942390-00-8 (hc)   ISBN 978-1-942390-01-5 (sc)

    1. Plays on words—Juvenile literature. 2. English language—Compound words—Juvenile literature. 3. English language—Phonetics—Juvenile literature. 4. Tongue twisters—Juvenile literature. [1. Plays on words. 2. English language—Compound words. 3. English language—Phonetics. 4. Tongue twisters.] I. George, Lindsay Barrett, illustrator. II. Babjak, Jim. III. Title.

P304.A35 2016   428.1
                QBI15-600078

Hi, parents and teachers!

We wanted to take a moment to welcome you (or welcome you back if you're a fan of *How Much Wood Could a Woodchuck Chuck?*) to another meaningful volume in our mission to make literacy fun through words, pictures, and music. Be it *How Much Wood Could a Woodchuck Chuck?*, which employs compound words and inverse descriptives, *Oh No, Domino!*, an early concept book featuring circles and repetitive phrasing, our chapter book *Mommy's Having a Watermelon*, filled cover to cover with contextual puns, any of our other books and CDs, or the *Woodchuck*-inspired and award-winning game *Compound It All!*, you'll find plenty to pore over and return to with kids (and though you won't admit it out loud, you'll probably spend some time looking at it when you're alone, too; we've been there).

We thought we'd give you some insights into how this package can enhance story time and be used as a learning tool, as well. The rhymes all come from compound words (except for toucan; that one is just for fun). Inside the book you will find a CD that has the song, rendered in two ways: first, with vocals, and next, as an instrumental version, so that you and your child or children can make up rhymes and compound words, and be silly at home or in the classroom. You will also find the music to the first two phrases printed in the book, complete with lyrics, so that you can sing it with or without the CD. What will we think of next?

We all had a blast making this book and CD for you, and we hope that comes through...we think it does. We also hope you use it as a fun educational tool! After all, the more fun learning is, the easier it is to learn!

Thanks again, and peace!

DISCOVERING TWO UNDISCOVERED ILLUSTRATORS

We had all of the artists in place—twelve of them!—when right in the middle of the project, one had to drop out. We understood but were left with a hole to fill. We thought hard about simply reaching into our bag of illustrators. Ultimately, however, we decided this was an opportunity to introduce you to a new artist...but how? We decided after lots of thought and conversation that a contest was the best way. We let folks know, primarily on social media, that we were looking for an artist, and word spread quickly! We received lots of entries, and it was so tough to make our choice, we decided to choose two and have one do the *Can You?* spread.

We are proud to introduce you to both Christee Curran-Bauer and Symone Banks, and we know you'll be seeing lots more of their fabulous work. Welcome to the wonderful world of picture books, illustrators!

The Rainfall Handbook
by Russell Goodwin

How much snow could a snowshoe shoo
if a snowshoe could shoo snow?

As much snow as a snowshoe could
if a snowshoe could shoo snow!

As much tea as a
teaspoon could
if a teaspoon could
spoon tea!

How much jelly could a jellyfish fish
if a jellyfish could fish jelly?

As much jelly as a jellyfish could
if a jellyfish could fish jelly!

How much honey could
a honeycomb comb
if a honeycomb could comb honey?

As much honey as a honeycomb could
if a honeycomb could comb honey!

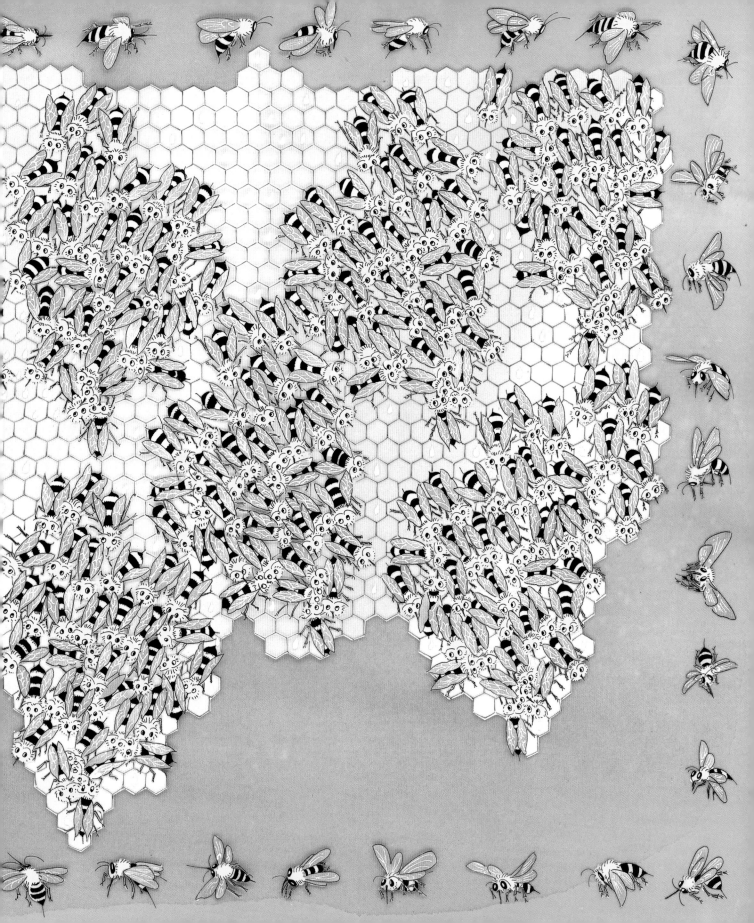

How much milk could a milkshake shake
if a milkshake could shake milk?

As much milk as a milkshake could
if a milkshake could shake milk!

How much paint could a paintbrush brush
if a paintbrush could brush paint?
As much paint as a paintbrush could

if a paintbrush could brush paint!

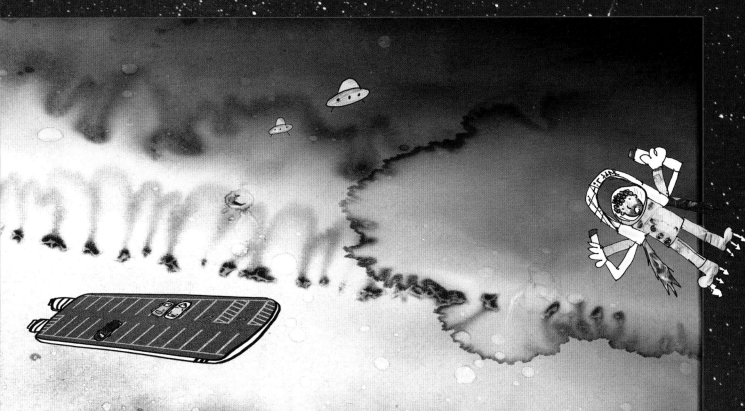

As much space as a spaceship could
if a spaceship could ship space!

How much rock could a rockhopper hop
if a rockhopper could hop a rock?

How much ice could an ice cream scream
if an ice cream could scream "ice"?

As much ice as an ice cream could
if an ice cream could scream "ice"!

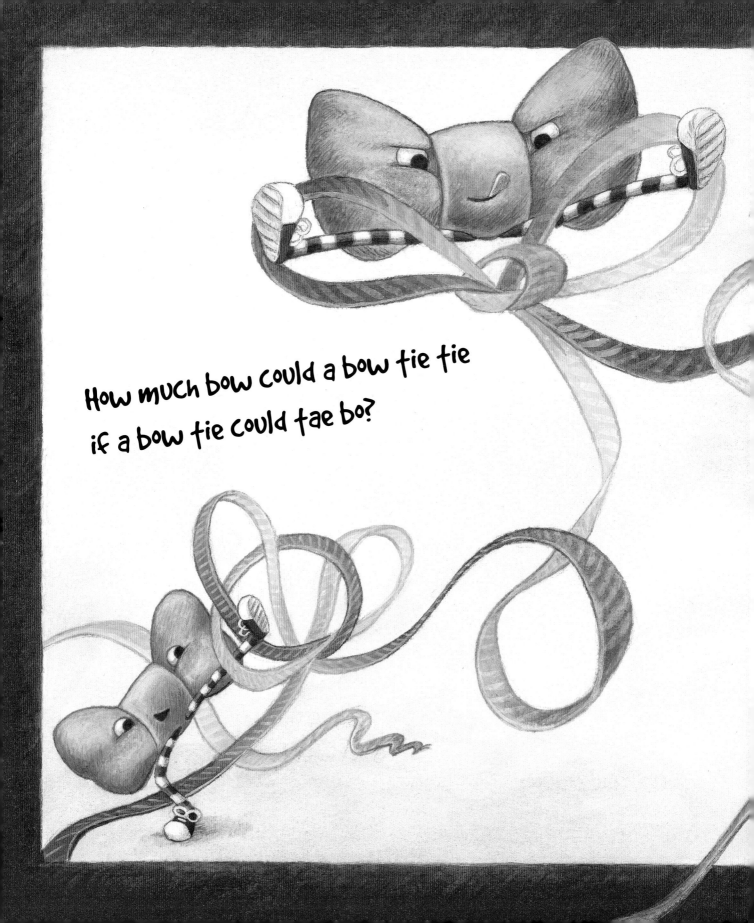

How much bow could a bow tie tie
if a bow tie could tae bo?

As much bow as a bow tie could if a bow tie could tae bo!

How much two could a toucan can
if a toucan could can two?

As much two as a toucan can
if a toucan could can two!

MEET THE ARTISTS!

LINDSAY BARRETT GEORGE is an award-winning and well-decorated artist, having been honored for her books and artistic talents over the many years. Lindsay began her career in children's books as a designer at a New York City publisher. She combined a fine arts background with her graphic design experience to produce books that make her favorite animals come alive. Lindsay has doodled the animals outside her homes in New Jersey, New York, Massachusetts, and Wisconsin, but is presently doodling the critters outside her 1898 red brick schoolhouse in White Mills, PA. Lindsay lives with her husband, a sweet mini-Dachshund, a big brown dog, five cats, and a very handsome duck.

MEGAN HALSEY has illustrated nearly 45 books for children, some of which she also wrote. In addition to her accomplishments in the field of children's books, her editorial work for grown-ups has appeared in major publications, including *Family Circle* and *The Boston Globe*. Her creations can also be seen in wall art, frames, textiles, bookmarks, and greeting cards. Megan taught at Pratt Institute for ten years and is currently a faculty member in the MFA Program for Working Professionals at Marywood University in Scranton, PA.

A former New Yorker, Megan now lives in the charming town of Lansdowne, PA, where she serves on the borough-appointed arts board and is co-chair of The Lansdowne Arts Festival, a three-day celebration of music and art. To learn more about Megan, visit www.MeganHalsey.com.

ASHLEY WOLFF is the author and/or illustrator of over 60 children's picture books, including *Baby Bear Sees Blue, Baby Beluga, Stella and Roy Go Camping, The Wild Little Horse, Who Took the Cookies from the Cookie Jar?, When Lucy Goes Out Walking, I Call My Grandma Nana, Compost Stew,* and the beloved Miss Bindergarten series. Her books have won numerous state and national awards. For 30 years one of Ashley's favorite pastimes has been traveling to schools all over the U.S., speaking to children about writing, drawing, and using their imaginations to help them find their own paths to the future. She lives and works in San Francisco, Vermont, and Virginia. For more information go to www.ashleywolff.com.

DEMI is the award-winning author of over 130 bestselling children's books. Her titles have sold over half a million copies. *The Empty Pot* was selected by former First Lady Barbara Bush as one of the books to read on the ABC Radio Network program *Mrs. Bush's Story Time*, sponsored by the Children's Literacy Initiative. It was also named a "Teachers' Top 100 Books for Children" in a poll by the National Education Association. Demi's book *Ghandi* was named a *New York Times* Best Illustrated Book and received an Oppenheim Toy Portfolio Platinum Award. In addition, she represented the United States at the First International Children's Book Conference in Beijing, China. She lives with her husband in Washington State.

RALPH MASIELLO was born, raised, and still resides in the state of Massachusetts, where he lives with his daughters Alexa and Talia. A graduate of the Rhode Island School of Design, Ralph has illustrated for magazines, newspapers, and books, created posters and prints, and shown his fine art paintings in galleries throughout the world. Beginning with *The Icky Bug Alphabet Book* in 1986, Ralph has become internationally known for the children's books he has written and illustrated. He developed the successful How to Draw book series, the most recent being *Ralph Masiello's Alien Drawing Book*.

WENDY ANDERSON HALPERIN has illustrated over 30 children's books and authored and illustrated three. She loves to draw the natural world and the human experience. Her books have been featured in *USA Today* and *The New York Times*. Most of her books are watercolor over pencil. Wendy created the award-winning program Drawing Children Into Reading, a drawing program instructing teachers of students aged 4-7 how to draw. Drawing Children Into Peace, another project Wendy works on, is designed to teach children about peace, peacemakers, and peace symbols and to provide a place where children can express their own ideas about peace. She lives in South Haven, MI, with her husband, author and storyteller John Mooy. They have three children, all living in New York City.

KEVIN KAMMERAAD loves to perform, write, draw, sing, make things, and wonder about possibilities. He is an award-winning artist, performer, and children's author of many books and CDs who loves to collaborate with other artists. Each year, he visits many schools, libraries, festivals, and conferences to inspire active imaginations through poetry, puppetry, music, and movement. He and his family live in Grand Rapids, MI. Visit www.kevinkammeraad.com for more information.

Photo by Karl Blessing

PAT CUMMINGS is the author and/or illustrator of over 35 books for young readers. She also edited the award-winning series *Talking With Artists*, which profiles prominent children's book illustrators. Pat makes appearances at schools, universities, and organizations. She also teaches Children's Book classes at Pratt Institute and Parsons, and conducts a summer Children's Book Boot Camp, where writers and illustrators meet with editors and art directors from major publishing houses. Pat serves on the boards of The Authors Guild, The Authors League Fund, SCBWI, and The Eric Carle Museum of Picture Book Art, and is a member of The Writers Guild of America, East. Her latest book, *Beauty and the Beast* (HarperCollins, 2014), was translated from the original French and retold by her husband Chuku Lee. Visit www.patcummings.com.

DAR (HOSTA) is an artist who does many things. She is a painter of trees, a writer and illustrator of children's picture books, a designer, a teacher of both children and adults, a speaker on creativity and education, and a creativity coach. Dar is the daughter of an artist, and her exploration in visual arts has been lifelong and self-motivated; her two favorite traditional mediums are cut paper collage and acrylic on canvas. She lives in New Hope, PA, in a quaint, old house surrounded by trees and lots and lots of frogs. For more about Dar, go to www.darsworld.com.

LEEZA HERNANDEZ grew up on an island off the south coast of England. She is the illustrator of *Never Play Music Right Next to the Zoo* (S&S), written by John Lithgow, the Eat Your Homework series (Charlesbridge), written by Ann McCallum, and is both author and illustrator of *Cat Napped!* and *Dog Gone!* (G.P. Putnam's Sons). Her love of line and cheeky humor in illustration is inspired by Roald Dahl and Quentin Blake books such as *George's Marvellous Medicine* and *Fantastic Mr. Fox*. Today she juggles her time between her family, art studio, and working as an art director for a local magazine. She has never owned a hamster or a pig—not real ones, anyway! Visit www.leezaworks.com.

CHRISTEE CURRAN–BAUER, one of our two contest winners, was born in New Jersey and received her BFA in Communications Design from Pratt Institute in Brooklyn. She loves drawing, reading, and New York pizza, in that order. Currently, she lives in Hawaii (where, thankfully, there is also pizza) with her husband who is stationed at Pearl Harbor. It's a mystery where they will move next, but she looks forward to the adventure! You can check out Christee at her website: christeecurranillustration.carbonmade.com or her blog: christeewithadoublee.blogspot.com.

KIM ADLERMAN is the author/illustrator of *Oh No, Domino!*, illustrator of both *Africa Calling, Nighttime Falling* and *Rock-a-bye Baby*, and the co-author of many books with her husband Danny, including *It's Raining, It's Pouring* under the pen name Kin Eagle. Most recently, Kim created *Compound It All!*, the compound word-building game which came to Kim in a dream subconsciously inspired by *How Much Wood Could a Woodchuck Chuck?*, in which she was a contributing illustrator.

Kim lives in New Jersey with her family, including a cat and dog. For more information about Kim and her works, check out www.dannyandkim.com.

Photo by Chloe Sklans

SYMONE BANKS, our second contest winner, hails from Piscataway, New Jersey. A graduate of the duCret School of Art, she is inspired by everyday surroundings, fantasy, and the supernatural world, including visions and dreams. Currently, Symone works on various projects as a freelancer. This is her first children's picture book. To create the *Can You?* spread, as it has come to be known, Symone first rendered a base plate in guache, which can be seen at the left. Then, several of the other illustrators of this book—Kim, Leeza, Kevin, Megan, Dar, and Ashley—gave us smaller pieces which Kim integrated into Symone's piece, the result of which can be seen full-size elsewhere in the book. In it, you will find more than 45 compound words...some are easy, and some are tricky. Just flip the page for a complete list. If you find others we missed, email us at: info@dannyandkim.com.

MEET the AUTHOR and MUSICIANS!

DANNY ADLERMAN has made many, many things in his life, including music, books, games, and a mess. His many CDs were made with a whole lot of friends, and Danny feels he is a better musican thanks to them. He also loves writing books, and he has had help from oodles of friends, most especially Kim, his beautiful wife and partner. Kim and Danny also recently co-created a word game called *Compound It All!* The messes, however, he tends to make on his own. Danny and Kim live somewhere in New Jersey. Together they made a home, where their children and various pets can often be found. You can like their Facebook page at: www.facebook.com/DannyandKim.

JIM BABJAK began playing guitar at age 12. His interest in music led him to become a founding member, songwriter, and lead guitarist of the world-renowned rock group The Smithereens. The Smithereens have sold more than 4 million albums worldwide and have appeared on many television shows including *Saturday Night Live, The Tonight Show with Jay Leno,* and MTV's *Unplugged*. Their music can be heard in numerous movies and soundtracks, such as *Bull Durham, Backdraft, Time Cop, Boys Don't Cry,* and *Harold & Kumar Go to White Castle*. The Smithereens still record and tour after almost 35 years. You can hear more of Jim's music for kids and families on *One Size Fits All* and *Listen UP!*, which he recorded with Danny. Learn more about Jim at www.jimbabjak.com.

A Toucan Can Can You?

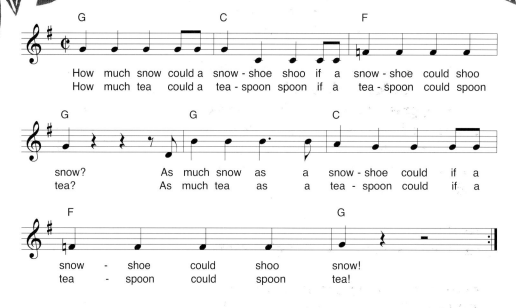

How much snow could a snow-shoe shoo if a snow-shoe could shoo
How much tea could a tea-spoon spoon if a tea-spoon could spoon

snow? As much snow as a snow-shoe could if a
tea? As much tea as a tea-spoon could if a

snow - shoe could shoo snow!
tea - spoon could spoon tea!

3. How much jelly could a jellyfish fish if a jellyfish could fish jelly?
   As much jelly as a jellyfish could if a jellyfish could fish jelly!

4. How much honey could a honeycomb comb if a honeycomb could comb honey?
   As much honey as a honeycomb could if a honeycomb could comb honey!

5. How much milk could a milkshake shake if a milkshake could shake milk?
   As much milk as a milkshake could if a milkshake could shake milk!

6. How much paint could a paintbrush brush if a paintbrush could brush paint?
   As much paint as a paintbrush could if a paintbrush could brush paint!

7. How much space could a spaceship ship if a spaceship could ship space?
   As much space as a spaceship could if a spaceship could ship space!

8. How much rock could a rockhopper hop if a rockhopper could hop a rock?
   As much rock as a rockhopper could if a rockhopper could hop a rock!

9. How much ice could an ice cream scream if an ice cream could scream "ice"?
   As much ice as an ice cream could if an ice cream could scream "ice"!

10. How much ham could a hamster stir if a hamster could stir ham?
    As much ham as a hamster could if a hamster could stir ham!

11. How much bow could a bow tie tie if a bow tie could tae bo?
    As much bow as a bow tie could if a bow tie could tae bo!

12. How much two could a toucan can if a toucan could can two?
    As much two as a toucan can if a toucan could can two!

Can you?